Cook Memorial Library
93 Main Street
Tamworth, NH 03886

P9-CLU-543

6/5/02

Little Squirrel's Special Nest

Claude Clément
Adapted by Patricia Jensen
Illustrations by Bernadette Pons

Reader's Digest Kids
Pleasantville, N.Y.— Montreal

Little Squirrel was always busy working
by herself. One day she was preparing her nest
for winter when her friends showed up.

"Come with us," said the hedgehog. "We're
going to gather nuts and berries."

"No, thank you," said Little Squirrel. "I still
have lots to do before my nest is ready."

"We'll help you!" said the mouse. "It's more
fun to do things together than alone."

Little Squirrel shook her head. "No thanks,"
she said. "I'd rather work by myself."

Later, the dormouse saw Little Squirrel carrying an armful of nuts.

"Those look heavy," said the dormouse. "May I help you carry them?"

"I can do it myself," panted Little Squirrel.

"Suit yourself," said the dormouse. "I'm off to play with the others."

At last, Little Squirrel's nest was complete. All by herself, she had gathered her winter's supply of nuts and lined the nest with pieces of soft, warm fabric. Exhausted from the hard work, Little Squirrel curled up in her nest, and soon she fell fast asleep.

Winter arrived early the next morning. It snowed and snowed. Soon a thick white blanket covered the forest.

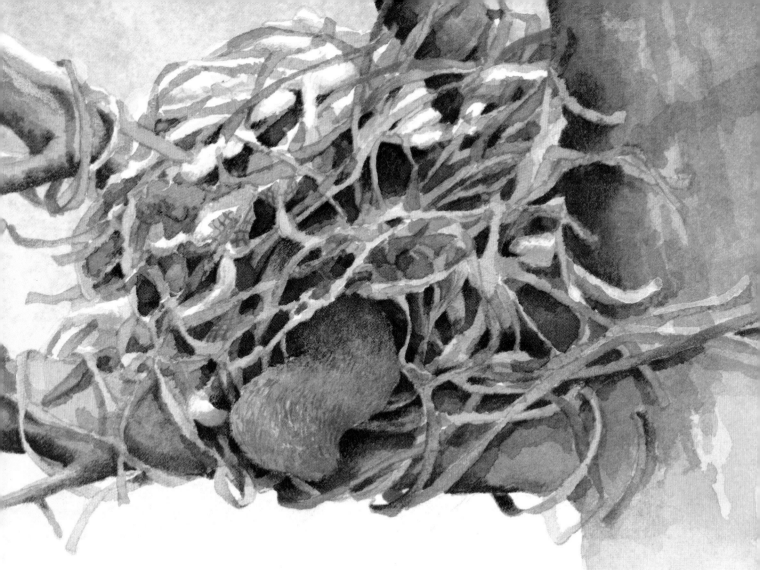

Little Squirrel slept soundly. She didn't even stir when a large bird perched near her nest. The bird stole the nuts and fabric scraps that Little Squirrel had collected. After robbing the nest of all its treasures, the bird flew away.

Little Squirrel woke up shivering.

"Why am I so cold?" she wondered. She looked around for her scraps of warm fabric. Then she noticed the hollow where she had stored her nuts.

"I've been robbed!" she cried. "How will I get through the winter without food to eat or a warm place to sleep?"

Little Squirrel ran down the tree and began to scurry around, looking for new supplies.

She saw the dormouse and the hedgehog tucked snugly in their nests, but found no nuts or scraps of cloth. The other forest animals had already gathered up everything.

"What will I do now?" Little Squirrel worried. Finally, she had an idea. "Maybe I can find what I need in the old barn." And off she went.

"Welcome to my winter home," said the mouse when she saw Little Squirrel. "I thought you were already asleep for the winter."

"I woke up to find my nest had been robbed," Little Squirrel explained. "Now I don't know what to do."

"How awful!" the mouse said. "If I had enough
room, I'd invite you to stay here with my family.
But at least I can give you some of our seeds."

"You're so helpful!" said Little Squirrel.

"Of course," said the mouse. "That's what
friends are for!"

Little Squirrel hurried back to the forest with the seeds. When she arrived at her tree, she saw the hedgehog and dormouse busily at work.

"Hello!" called the hedgehog. "We woke up a while ago and saw that you had been robbed. We're fixing up your nest with our own bits of cloth."

Little Squirrel watched for a minute and thought, "How nice it is to have help from friends." Then she scampered up the tree. "Let's all work on the nest together," she said.

Before long, the nest was finished.

"Thank you so much!" said Little Squirrel.

The hedgehog and dormouse climbed down from the tree. "Sleep well!" they called.

Little Squirrel wiggled into a comfortable position and gazed up at the sky. "When spring comes," she thought, "my friends and I can look for food together. We'll help the mouse take care of her family, too."

Then Little Squirrel wiggled deeper into the soft, warm nest and drifted off to sleep.

Squirrels build round nests with twigs, dead leaves, and bits of cloth. Sometimes squirrels rearrange and use nests that have been left behind by crows.

Squirrels feed on acorns, hazelnuts, walnuts, pine cone seeds, and chestnuts. They store them away for winter in secret hiding places.

When it begins to get cold, squirrels go to sleep for the winter. They wake up from time to time to nibble on food.